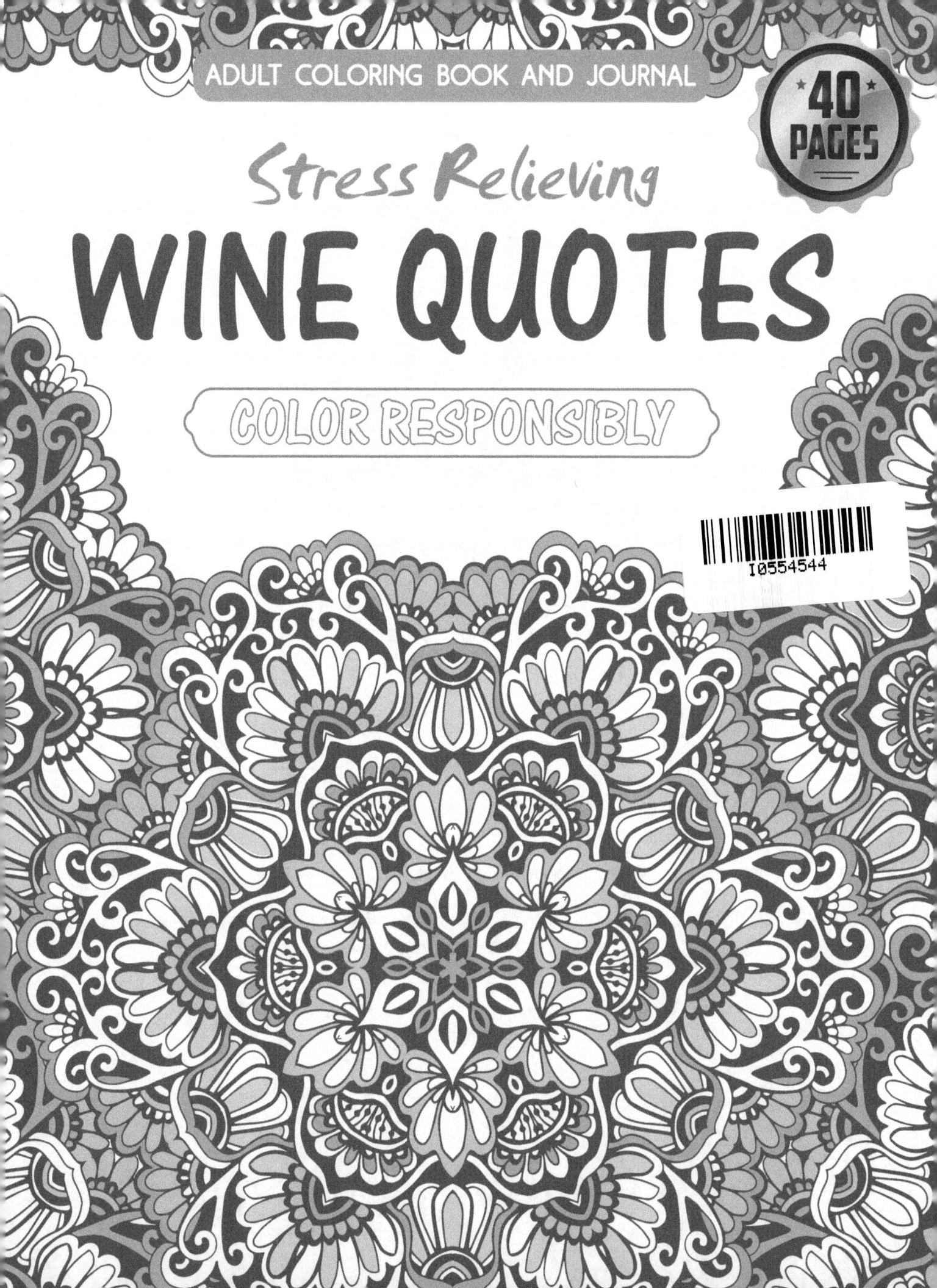

ADULT COLORING BOOK AND JOURNAL

40 PAGES

Stress Relieving

WINE QUOTES

COLOR RESPONSIBLY

By Matthew Fagin

ISBN 978-0-578-41787-5

Published by The CT Wine Review, LLC

Visit me at www.winesandtunes.com

To my wife Rosanna.

You always add color to my world!

And to Anna, Ivan, Elijah and Joshua, a colorful crew!

I love you all.

Name of Wine: _____

Region: _____

Type: _____ Vintage: _____

Vineyard: _____

Price: _____ Date: _____

Purchased/Received From: _____

Music Listened to: _____

Appearance: _____

Bouquet: _____

Taste: _____

Body: |_____|_____|
    Light   Medium   Full

Overall Rating:

☆ ☆ ☆ ☆ ☆

Additional Comments: _____
_____

Attach Wine Label Here

Name of Wine: _____

Region: _____

Type: _____ Vintage: _____

Vineyard: _____

Price: _____ Date: _____

Purchased/Received From: _____

Music Listened to: _____

Appearance: _____

Bouquet: _____

Taste: _____

Body: |——————————————|——————————————|

Light   Medium   Full

Overall Rating:

☆ ☆ ☆ ☆ ☆

Additional Comments: _____
_____

Attach Wine Label Here

Name of Wine: _____

Region: _____

Type: _____ Vintage: _____

Vineyard: _____

Price: _____ Date: _____

Purchased/Received From: _____

Music Listened to: _____

Appearance: _____

Bouquet: _____

Taste: _____

Body: |_____|_____|
      Light   Medium   Full

Overall Rating:

☆ ☆ ☆ ☆ ☆

Additional Comments: _____
_____

Attach Wine Label Here

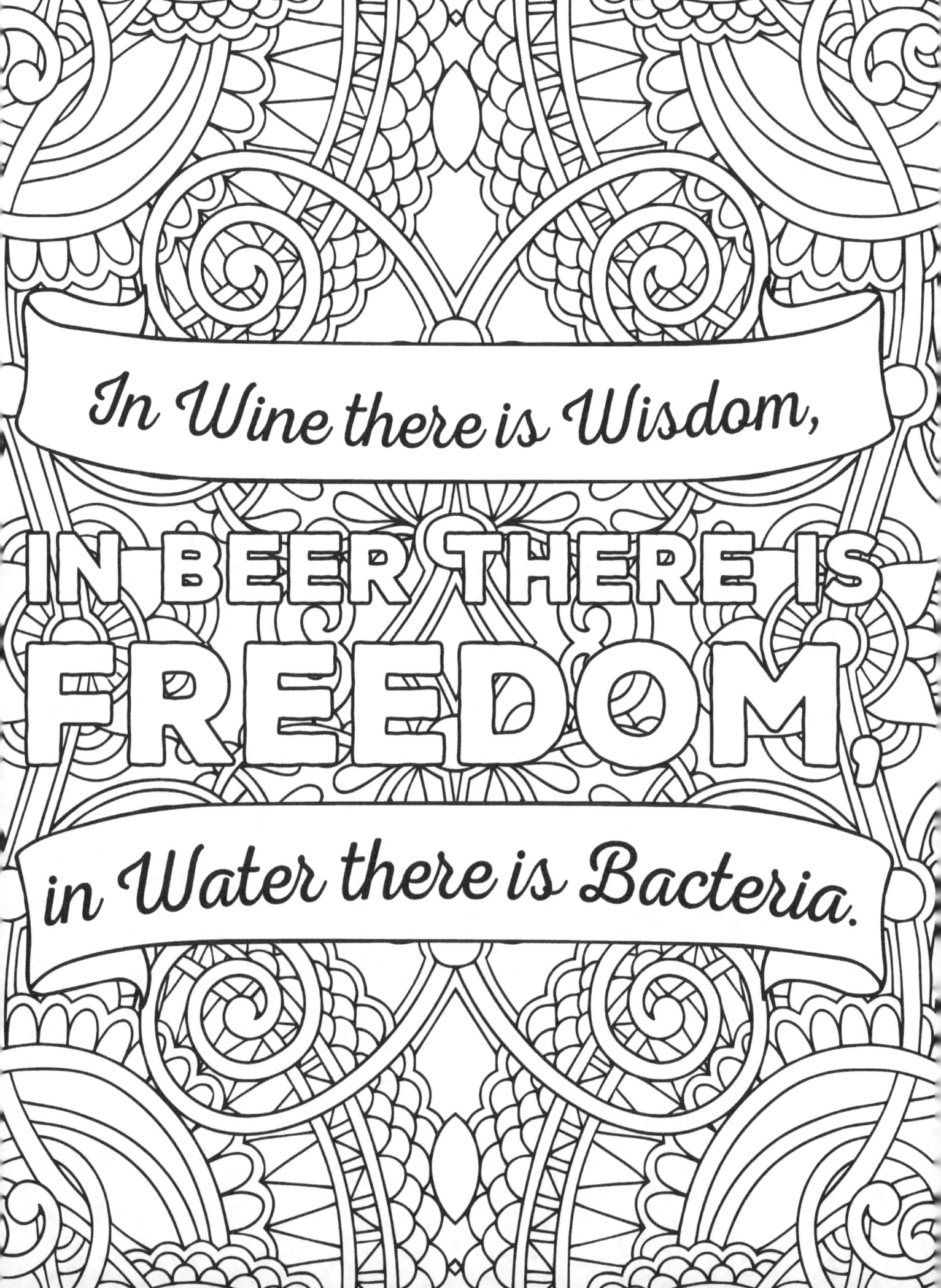

In Wine there is Wisdom, IN BEER THERE IS FREEDOM, in Water there is Bacteria.

Name of Wine: _____

Region: _____

Type: _____ Vintage: _____

Vineyard: _____

Price: _____ Date: _____

Purchased/Received From: _____

Music Listened to: _____

Appearance: _____

Bouquet: _____

Taste: _____

Body: ├─────────────────────┼─────────────────────┤

    Light   Medium   Full

Overall Rating:

☆ ☆ ☆ ☆ ☆

Additional Comments: _____

_____

Attach Wine Label Here

Name of Wine: _____

Region: _____

Type: _____ Vintage: _____

Vineyard: _____

Price: _____ Date: _____

Purchased/Received From: _____

Music Listened to: _____

Appearance: _____

Bouquet: _____

Taste: _____

Body: |_____|_____|

Light   Medium   Full

Overall Rating:

☆ ☆ ☆ ☆ ☆

Additional Comments: _____

_____

Attach Wine Label Here

I'm not having A GLASS OF WINE. I'm having six It's called a "tasting" and it's classy.

Name of Wine: _____

Region: _____

Type: _____ Vintage: _____

Vineyard: _____

Price: _____ Date: _____

Purchased/Received From: _____

Music Listened to: _____

Appearance: _____

Bouquet: _____

Taste: _____

Body: ├─────────────────┼─────────────────┤

Light   Medium   Full

Overall Rating:

☆ ☆ ☆ ☆ ☆

Additional Comments: _____

_____

Attach Wine Label Here

The first thing on my Bucket list is to fill the Bucket with wine.

Name of Wine: _____

Region: _____

Type: _____ Vintage: _____

Vineyard: _____

Price: _____ Date: _____

Purchased/Received From: _____

Music Listened to: _____

Appearance: _____

Bouquet: _____

Taste: _____

Body: |——————————————————|——————————————————|

    Light   Medium   Full

Overall Rating:

☆ ☆ ☆ ☆ ☆

Additional Comments: _____
_____

Attach Wine Label Here

Name of Wine: _____

Region: _____

Type: _____ Vintage: _____

Vineyard: _____

Price: _____ Date: _____

Purchased/Received From: _____

Music Listened to: _____

Appearance: _____

Bouquet: _____

Taste: _____

Body: |—————————————————————|—————————————————————|

    Light   Medium   Full

Overall Rating:

☆ ☆ ☆ ☆ ☆

Additional Comments: _____

_____

⌐   ¬

Attach Wine Label Here

⌐   ¬

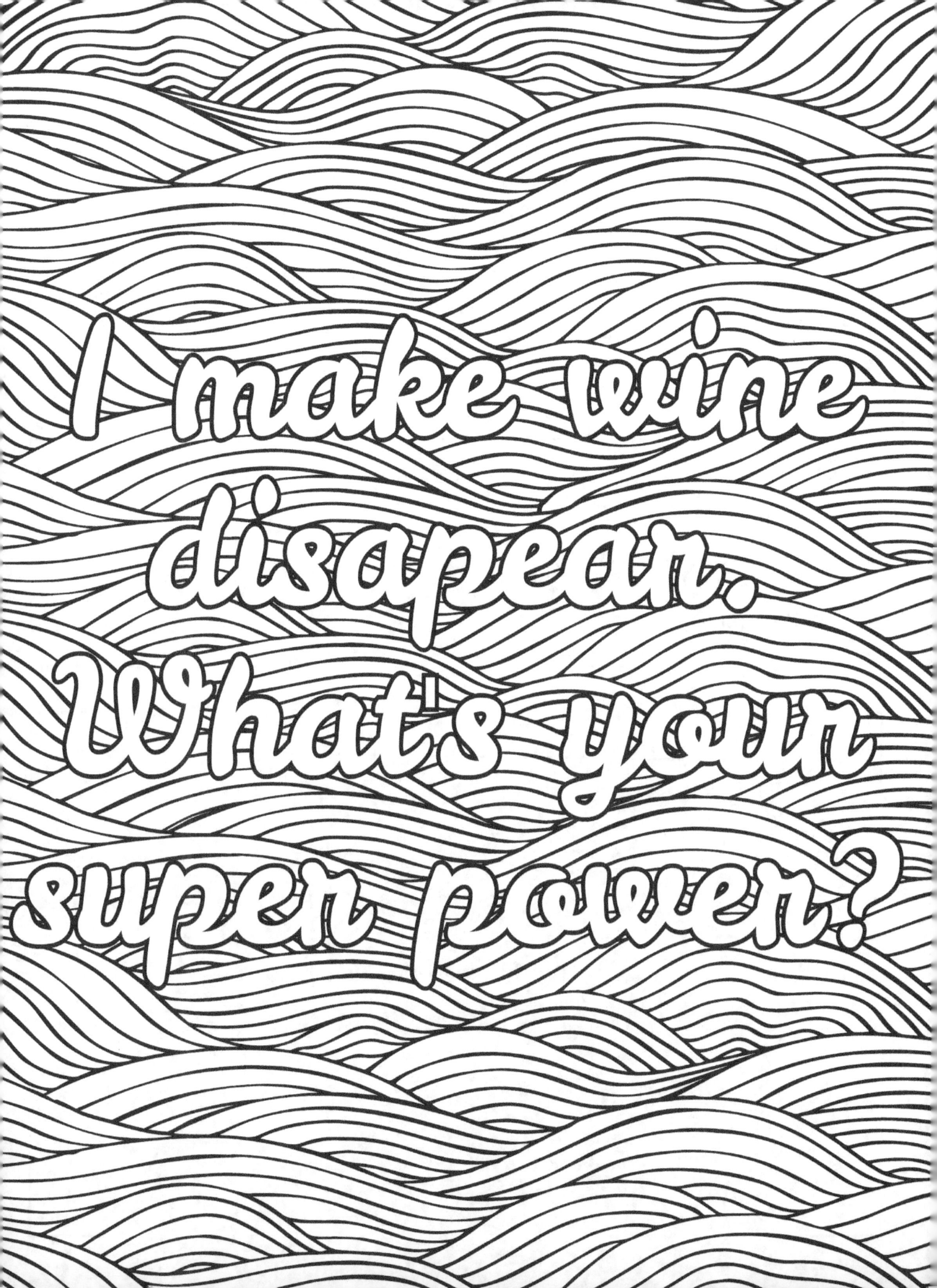

Name of Wine: _____

Region: _____

Type: _____ Vintage: _____

Vineyard: _____

Price: _____ Date: _____

Purchased/Received From: _____

Music Listened to: _____

Appearance: _____

Bouquet: _____

Taste: _____

Body: ├─────────────────────┼─────────────────────┤

Light   Medium   Full

Overall Rating:

☆ ☆ ☆ ☆ ☆

Additional Comments: _____

_____

Attach Wine Label Here

Name of Wine: _____

Region: _____

Type: _____ Vintage: _____

Vineyard: _____

Price: _____ Date: _____

Purchased/Received From: _____

Music Listened to: _____

Appearance: _____

Bouquet: _____

Taste: _____

Body: |——————————————|——————————————|

Light   Medium   Full

Overall Rating:

☆ ☆ ☆ ☆ ☆

Additional Comments: _____

_____

Attach Wine Label Here

Name of Wine: _____

Region: _____

Type: _____ Vintage: _____

Vineyard: _____

Price: _____ Date: _____

Purchased/Received From: _____

Music Listened to: _____

Appearance: _____

Bouquet: _____

Taste: _____

Body: ├─────────────────────────┼─────────────────────────┤

    Light   Medium   Full

Overall Rating:

☆ ☆ ☆ ☆ ☆

Additional Comments: _____

_____

Attach Wine Label Here

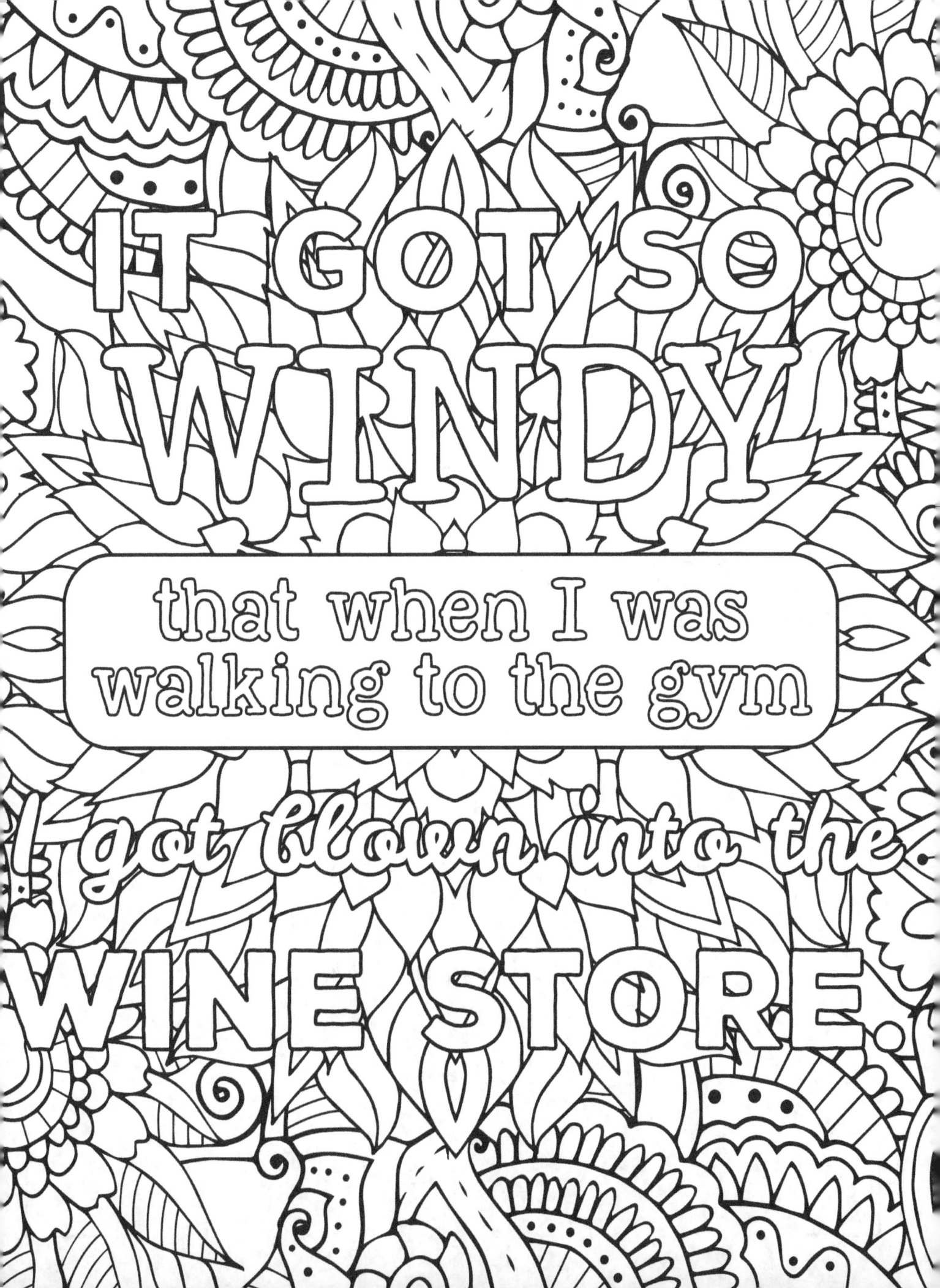

IT GOT SO **WINDY** that when I was walking to the gym I got blown into the **WINE STORE.**

Name of Wine: _____

Region: _____

Type: _____ Vintage: _____

Vineyard: _____

Price: _____ Date: _____

Purchased/Received From: _____

Music Listened to: _____

Appearance: _____

Bouquet: _____

Taste: _____

Body: |—————————————————|—————————————————|

   Light   Medium   Full

Overall Rating:

☆ ☆ ☆ ☆ ☆

Additional Comments: _____

_____

Attach Wine Label Here

IN VICTORY, you deserve Champagne. IN DEFEAT you need it.

Name of Wine: _____

Region: _____

Type: _____ Vintage: _____

Vineyard: _____

Price: _____ Date: _____

Purchased/Received From: _____

Music Listened to: _____

Appearance: _____

Bouquet: _____

Taste: _____

Body: |_____|_____|

Light   Medium   Full

Overall Rating:

☆ ☆ ☆ ☆ ☆

Additional Comments: _____
_____

Attach Wine Label Here

Name of Wine: _____

Region: _____

Type: _____ Vintage: _____

Vineyard: _____

Price: _____ Date: _____

Purchased/Received From: _____

Music Listened to: _____

Appearance: _____

Bouquet: _____

Taste: _____

Body: |—————————————|—————————————|

     Light   Medium   Full

Overall Rating:

☆ ☆ ☆ ☆ ☆

Additional Comments: _____

_____

Attach Wine Label Here

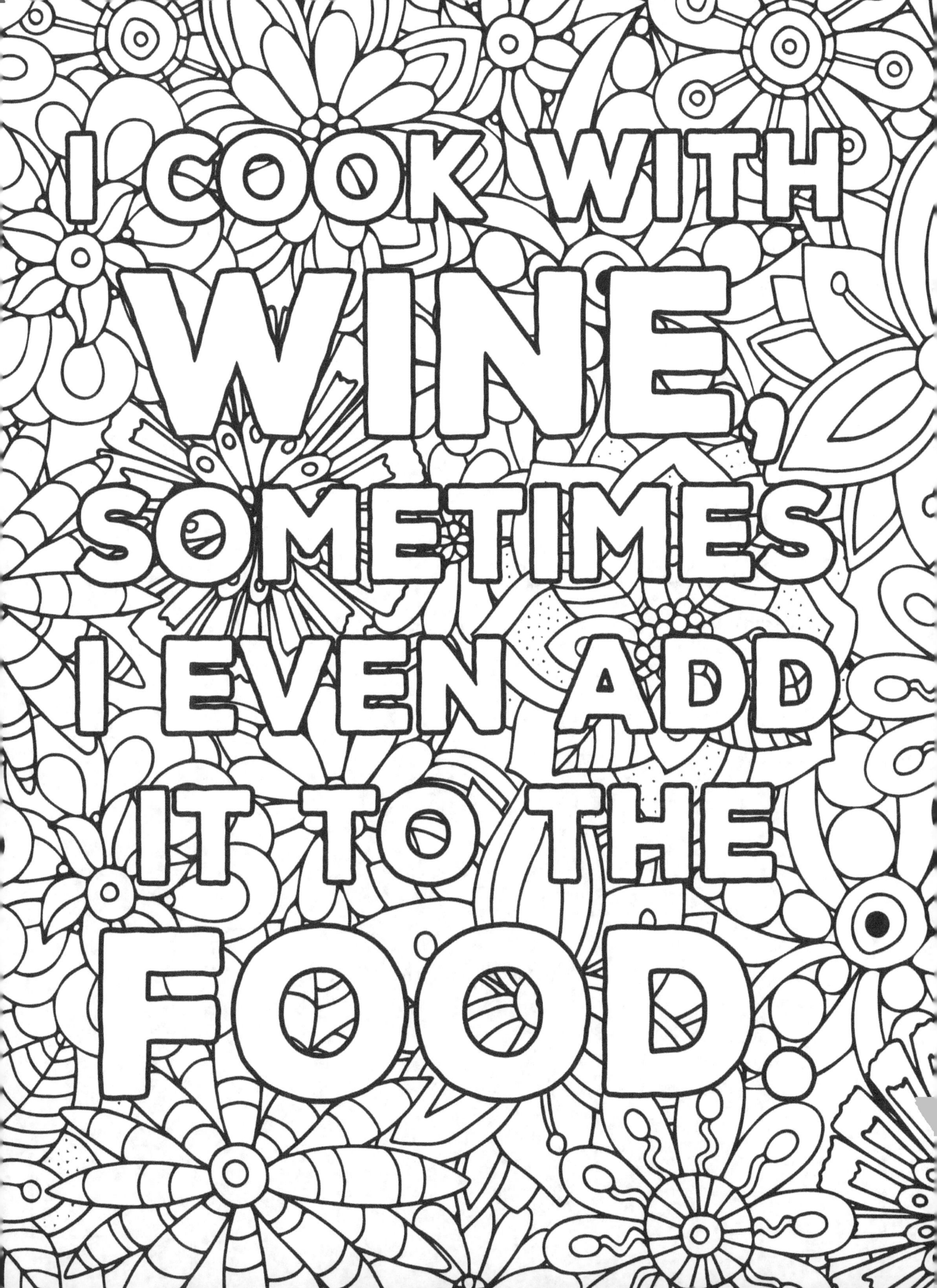

Name of Wine: _____

Region: _____

Type: _____ Vintage: _____

Vineyard: _____

Price: _____ Date: _____

Purchased/Received From: _____

Music Listened to: _____

Appearance: _____

Bouquet: _____

Taste: _____

Body:

|Light——————————Medium——————————Full|

Overall Rating:

☆ ☆ ☆ ☆ ☆

Additional Comments: _____
_____

Attach Wine Label Here

Name of Wine: _____

Region: _____

Type: _____ Vintage: _____

Vineyard: _____

Price: _____ Date: _____

Purchased/Received From: _____

Music Listened to: _____

Appearance: _____

Bouquet: _____

Taste: _____

Body: |——————————————————|——————————————————|

    Light   Medium   Full

Overall Rating:

☆ ☆ ☆ ☆ ☆

Additional Comments: _____

_____

Attach Wine Label Here

THEY SAY A GLASS OF WINE IS GOOD FOR YOU. SO TWO GLASSES MUST BE BETTER??

Name of Wine: _____

Region: _____

Type: _____ Vintage: _____

Vineyard: _____

Price: _____ Date: _____

Purchased/Received From: _____

Music Listened to: _____

Appearance: _____

Bouquet: _____

Taste: _____

Body: ├──────────────────┼──────────────────┤

Light   Medium   Full

Overall Rating:

☆ ☆ ☆ ☆ ☆

Additional Comments: _____
_____

Attach Wine Label Here

MEN ARE LIKE WINE - SOME TURN TO vinegar, BUT THE BEST improve with age.

Name of Wine: _____

Region: _____

Type: _____ Vintage: _____

Vineyard: _____

Price: _____ Date: _____

Purchased/Received From: _____

Music Listened to: _____

Appearance: _____

Bouquet: _____

Taste: _____

Body: |_____|_____|

      Light   Medium   Full

Overall Rating:

☆ ☆ ☆ ☆ ☆

Additional Comments: _____
_____

Attach Wine Label Here

Name of Wine: _____

Region: _____

Type: _____ Vintage: _____

Vineyard: _____

Price: _____ Date: _____

Purchased/Received From: _____

Music Listened to: _____

Appearance: _____

Bouquet: _____

Taste: _____

Body: |——————————————|——————————————|

Light   Medium   Full

Overall Rating:

☆ ☆ ☆ ☆ ☆

Additional Comments: _____
_____

Attach Wine Label Here

Name of Wine: _____

Region: _____

Type: _____   Vintage: _____

Vineyard: _____

Price: _____   Date: _____

Purchased/Received From: _____

Music Listened to: _____

Appearance: _____

Bouquet: _____

Taste: _____

Body: |—————————————|—————————————|

Light   Medium   Full

Overall Rating:

☆ ☆ ☆ ☆ ☆

Additional Comments: _____

_____

⌐   ¬

Attach Wine Label Here

∟   ⌐

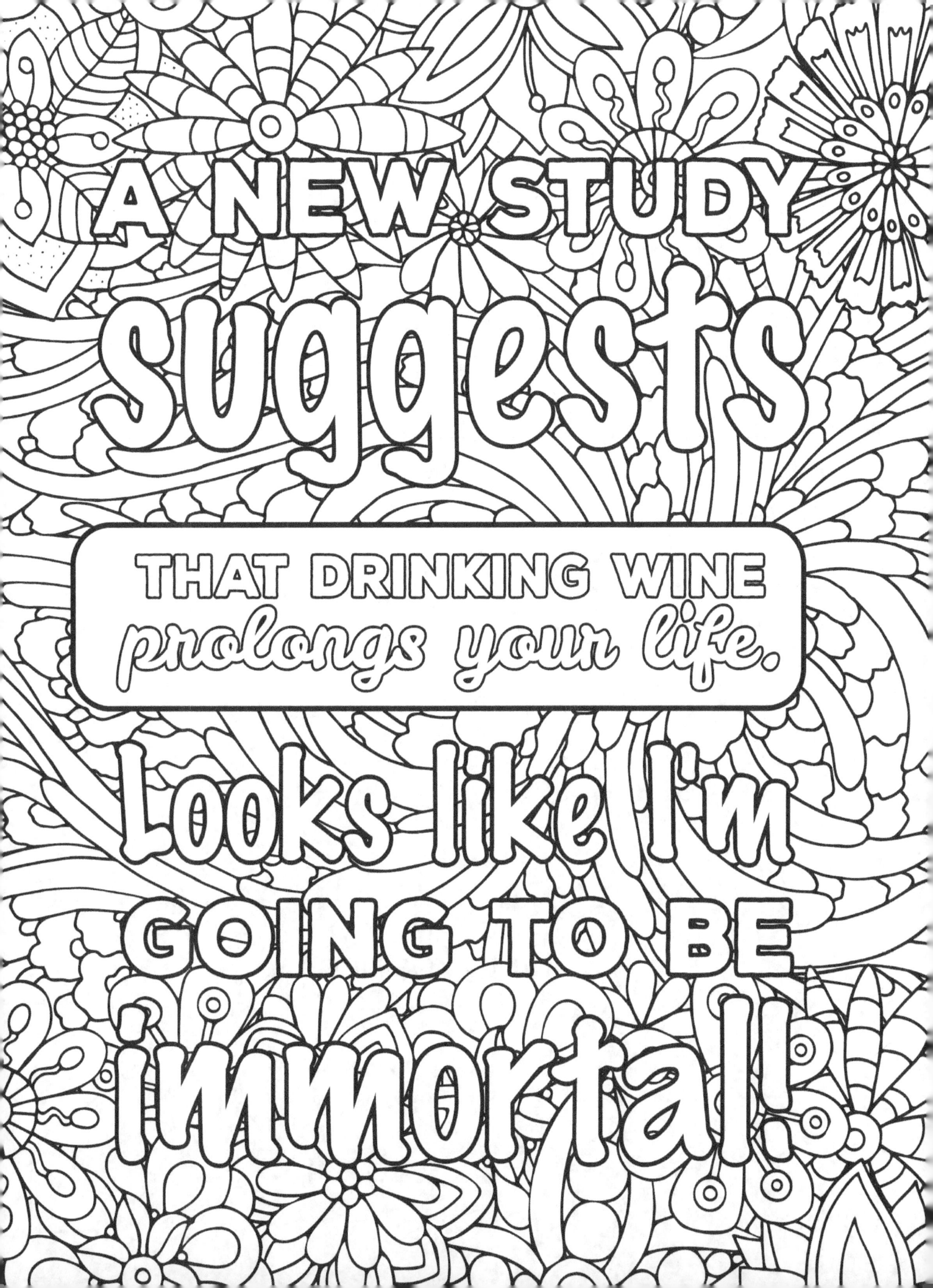

Name of Wine: _____

Region: _____

Type: _____ Vintage: _____

Vineyard: _____

Price: _____ Date: _____

Purchased/Received From: _____

Music Listened to: _____

Appearance: _____

Bouquet: _____

Taste: _____

Body: |_____|_____|

    Light   Medium   Full

Overall Rating:

☆ ☆ ☆ ☆ ☆

Additional Comments: _____
_____

Attach Wine Label Here

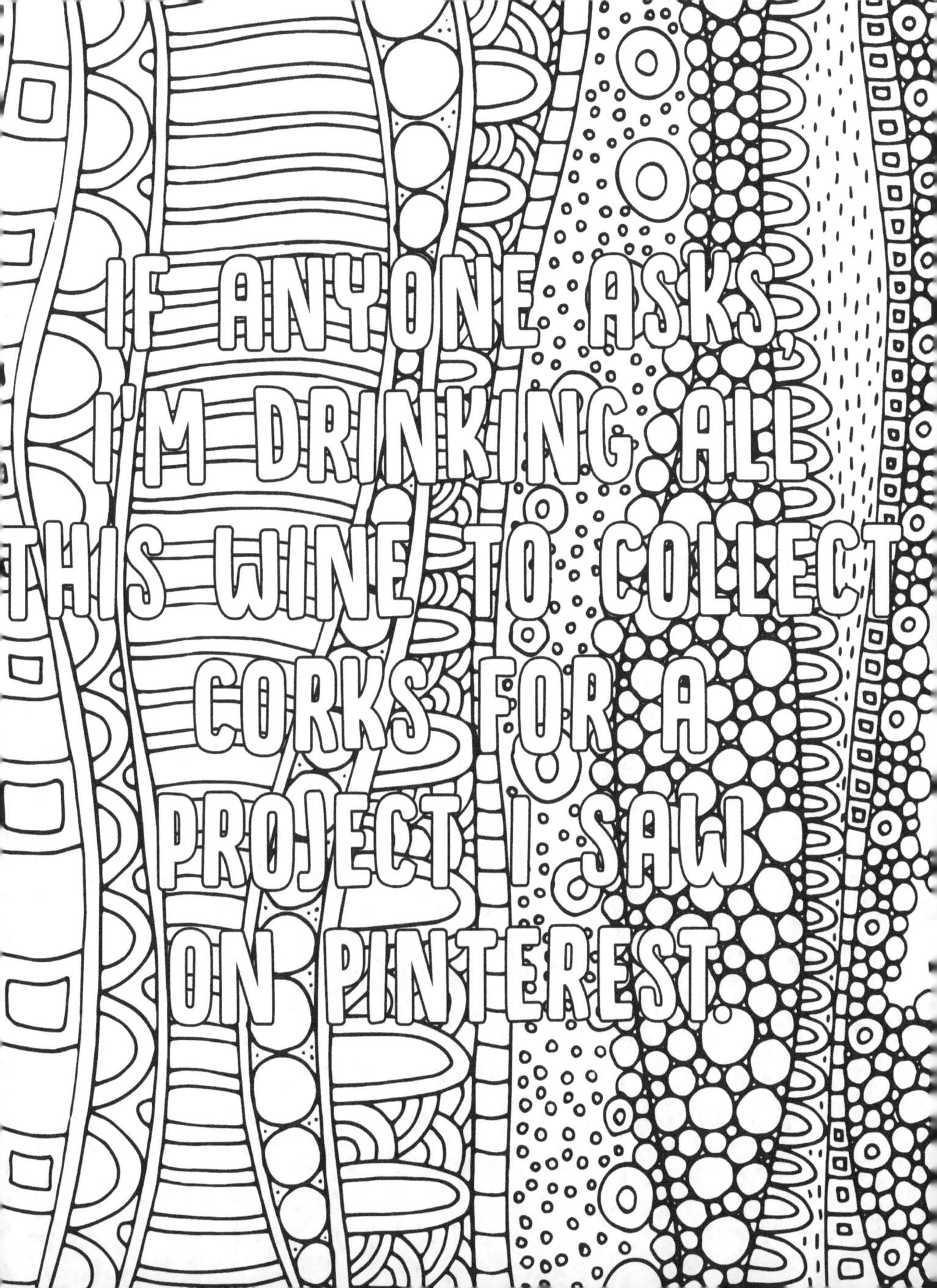

Name of Wine: _____

Region: _____

Type: _____ Vintage: _____

Vineyard: _____

Price: _____ Date: _____

Purchased/Received From: _____

Music Listened to: _____

Appearance: _____

Bouquet: _____

Taste: _____

Body: |_____|_____|

Light   Medium   Full

Overall Rating:

☆ ☆ ☆ ☆ ☆

Additional Comments: _____
_____

Attach Wine Label Here

Name of Wine: _____

Region: _____

Type: _____ Vintage: _____

Vineyard: _____

Price: _____ Date: _____

Purchased/Received From: _____

Music Listened to: _____

Appearance: _____

Bouquet: _____

Taste: _____

Body: |_____|_____|

Light   Medium   Full

Overall Rating:

☆ ☆ ☆ ☆ ☆

Additional Comments: _____
_____

Attach Wine Label Here

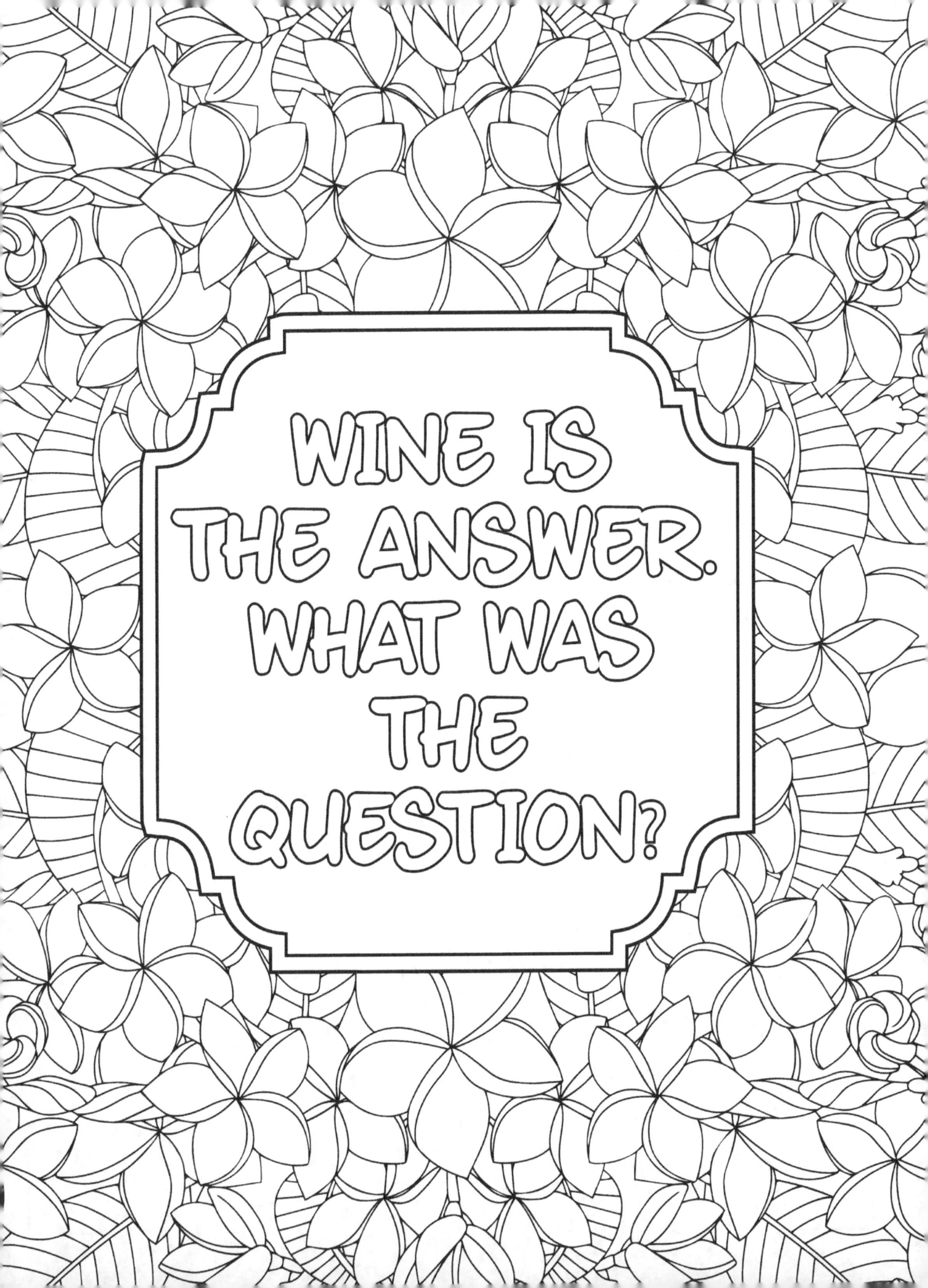

Name of Wine: _____

Region: _____

Type: _____ Vintage: _____

Vineyard: _____

Price: _____ Date: _____

Purchased/Received From: _____

Music Listened to: _____

Appearance: _____

Bouquet: _____

Taste: _____

Body: |————————————————|————————————————|

Light   Medium   Full

Overall Rating:

☆ ☆ ☆ ☆ ☆

Additional Comments: _____
_____

Attach Wine Label Here

I enjoy a glass of wine each night for its health benefits. The other glasses are for my witty comebacks and flawless dance moves.

Name of Wine: _____

Region: _____

Type: _____   Vintage: _____

Vineyard: _____

Price: _____   Date: _____

Purchased/Received From: _____

Music Listened to: _____

Appearance: _____

Bouquet: _____

Taste: _____

Body:

Light   Medium   Full

Overall Rating:

☆ ☆ ☆ ☆ ☆

Additional Comments: _____
_____

Attach Wine Label Here

WINE is to women as DUCT TAPE is to men... IT FIXES EVERYTHING

Name of Wine: _____

Region: _____

Type: _____ Vintage: _____

Vineyard: _____

Price: _____ Date: _____

Purchased/Received From: _____

Music Listened to: _____

Appearance: _____

Bouquet: _____

Taste: _____

Body: |—————————————————————————|—————————————————————————|

    Light   Medium   Full

Overall Rating:

☆ ☆ ☆ ☆ ☆

Additional Comments: _____

_____

Attach Wine Label Here

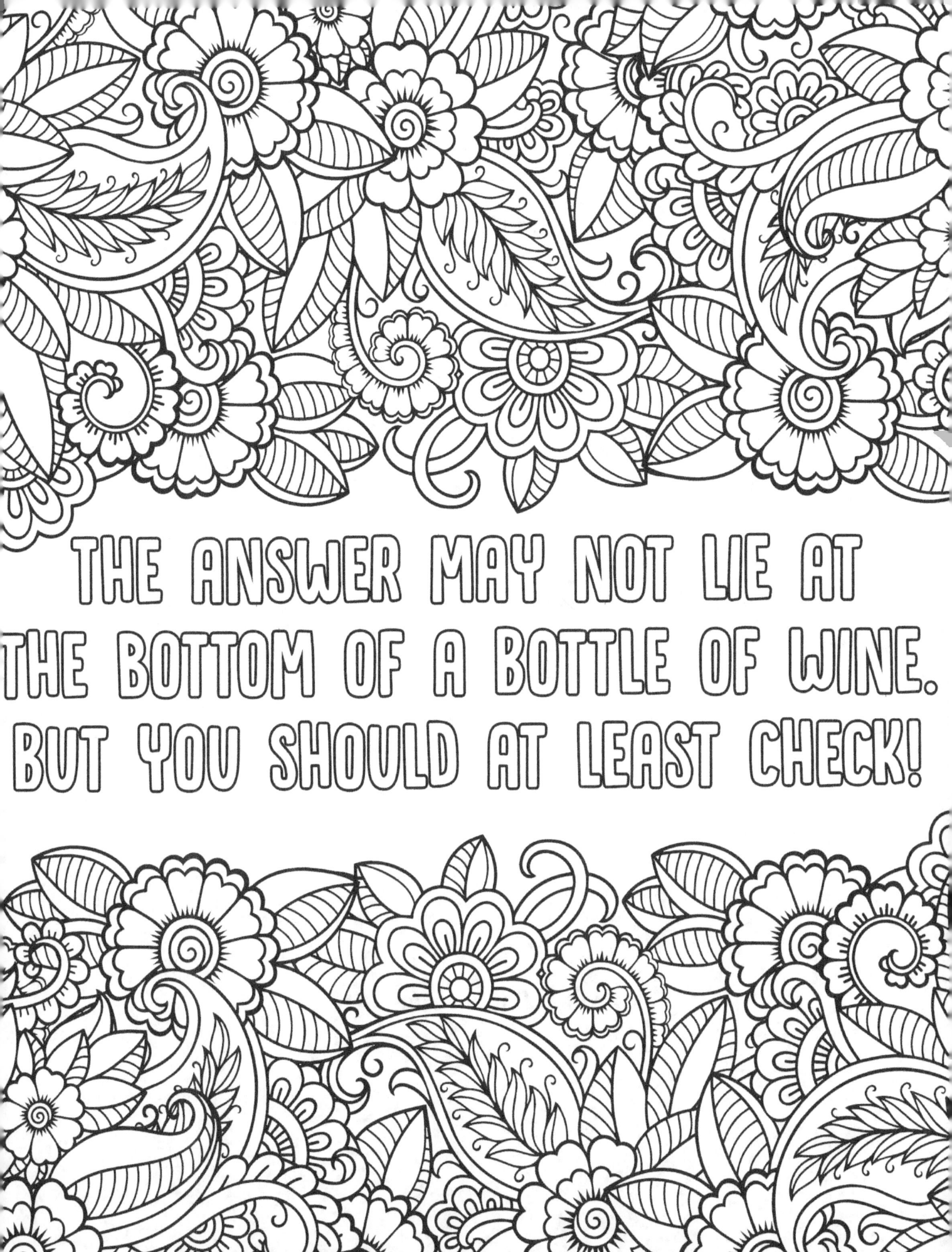

THE ANSWER MAY NOT LIE AT THE BOTTOM OF A BOTTLE OF WINE. BUT YOU SHOULD AT LEAST CHECK!

Name of Wine: _____

Region: _____

Type: _____ Vintage: _____

Vineyard: _____

Price: _____ Date: _____

Purchased/Received From: _____

Music Listened to: _____

Appearance: _____

Bouquet: _____

Taste: _____

Body: |_____|_____|
　　　Light　　　　　　　　　　Medium　　　　　　　　　Full

Overall Rating:

☆ ☆ ☆ ☆ ☆

Additional Comments: _____

_____

Attach Wine Label Here

Name of Wine: _____

Region: _____

Type: _____ Vintage: _____

Vineyard: _____

Price: _____ Date: _____

Purchased/Received From: _____

Music Listened to: _____

Appearance: _____

Bouquet: _____

Taste: _____

Body: |_____|_____|

    Light   Medium   Full

Overall Rating:

☆ ☆ ☆ ☆ ☆

Additional Comments: _____
_____

Attach Wine Label Here

Remember gentleman, it's not just
France we're fighting for,
it's Champagne!

Name of Wine: _____

Region: _____

Type: _____ Vintage: _____

Vineyard: _____

Price: _____ Date: _____

Purchased/Received From: _____

Music Listened to: _____

Appearance: _____

Bouquet: _____

Taste: _____

Body: |_____|_____|
   Light   Medium   Full

Overall Rating:

☆ ☆ ☆ ☆ ☆

Additional Comments: _____
_____

Attach Wine Label Here

Name of Wine: _____

Region: _____

Type: _____ Vintage: _____

Vineyard: _____

Price: _____ Date: _____

Purchased/Received From: _____

Music Listened to: _____

Appearance: _____

Bouquet: _____

Taste: _____

Body: |——————————————|——————————————|

     Light   Medium   Full

Overall Rating:

☆ ☆ ☆ ☆ ☆

Additional Comments: _____

_____

Attach Wine Label Here

I used to think WINE WAS BAD for me... so I gave up thinking.

Name of Wine: _____

Region: _____

Type: _____ Vintage: _____

Vineyard: _____

Price: _____ Date: _____

Purchased/Received From: _____

Music Listened to: _____

Appearance: _____

Bouquet: _____

Taste: _____

Body: |_____|_____|

Light   Medium   Full

Overall Rating:

☆ ☆ ☆ ☆ ☆

Additional Comments: _____
_____

Attach Wine Label Here

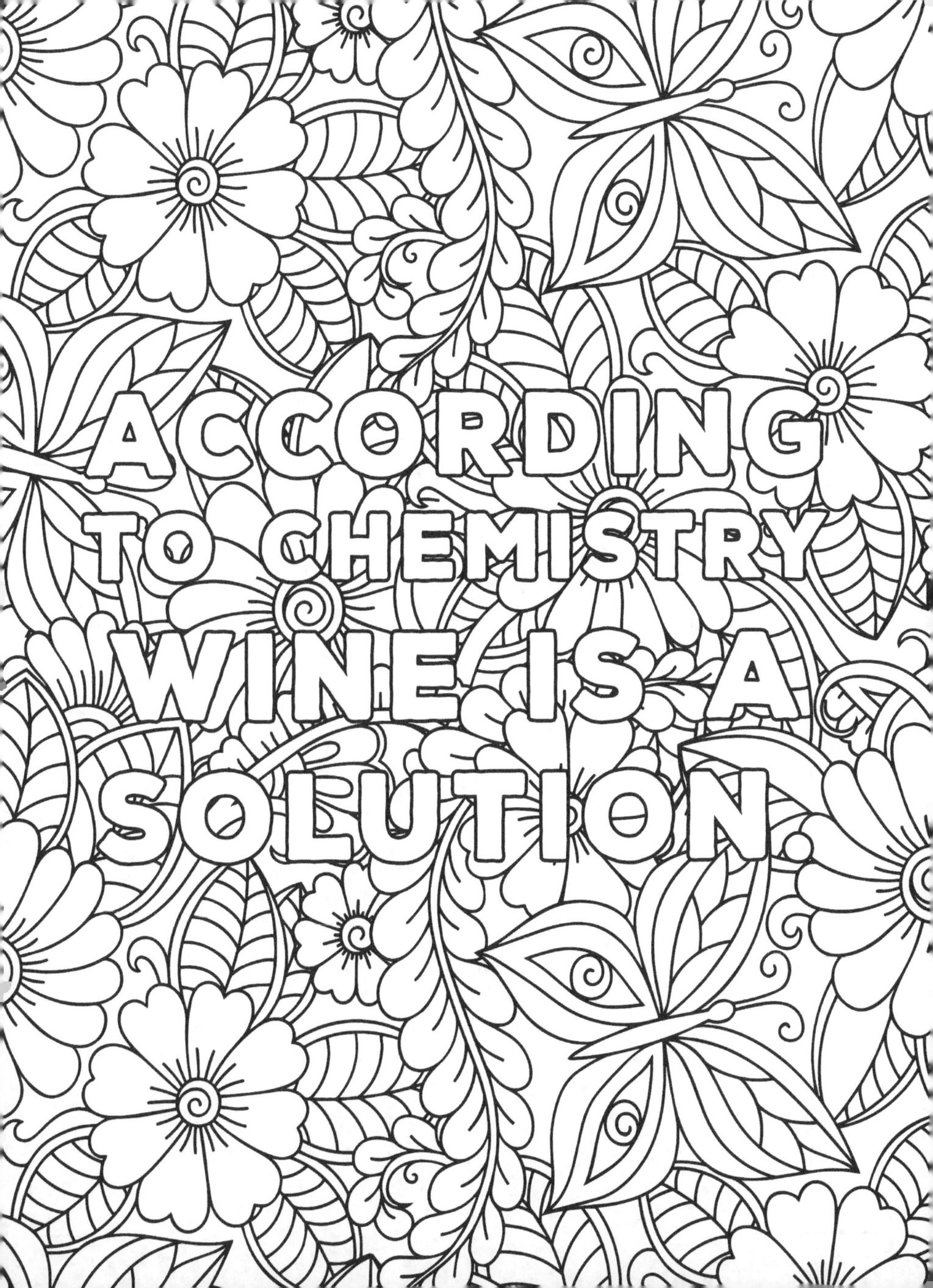

Name of Wine: _____

Region: _____

Type: _____ Vintage: _____

Vineyard: _____

Price: _____ Date: _____

Purchased/Received From: _____

Music Listened to: _____

Appearance: _____

Bouquet: _____

Taste: _____

Body: |_____|_____|

Light   Medium   Full

Overall Rating:

☆ ☆ ☆ ☆ ☆

Additional Comments: _____

_____

Attach Wine Label Here

Name of Wine: _____

Region: _____

Type: _____ Vintage: _____

Vineyard: _____

Price: _____ Date: _____

Purchased/Received From: _____

Music Listened to: _____

Appearance: _____

Bouquet: _____

Taste: _____

Body: |——————————————————|——————————————————|

    Light   Medium   Full

Overall Rating:

☆ ☆ ☆ ☆ ☆

Additional Comments: _____

_____

Attach Wine Label Here

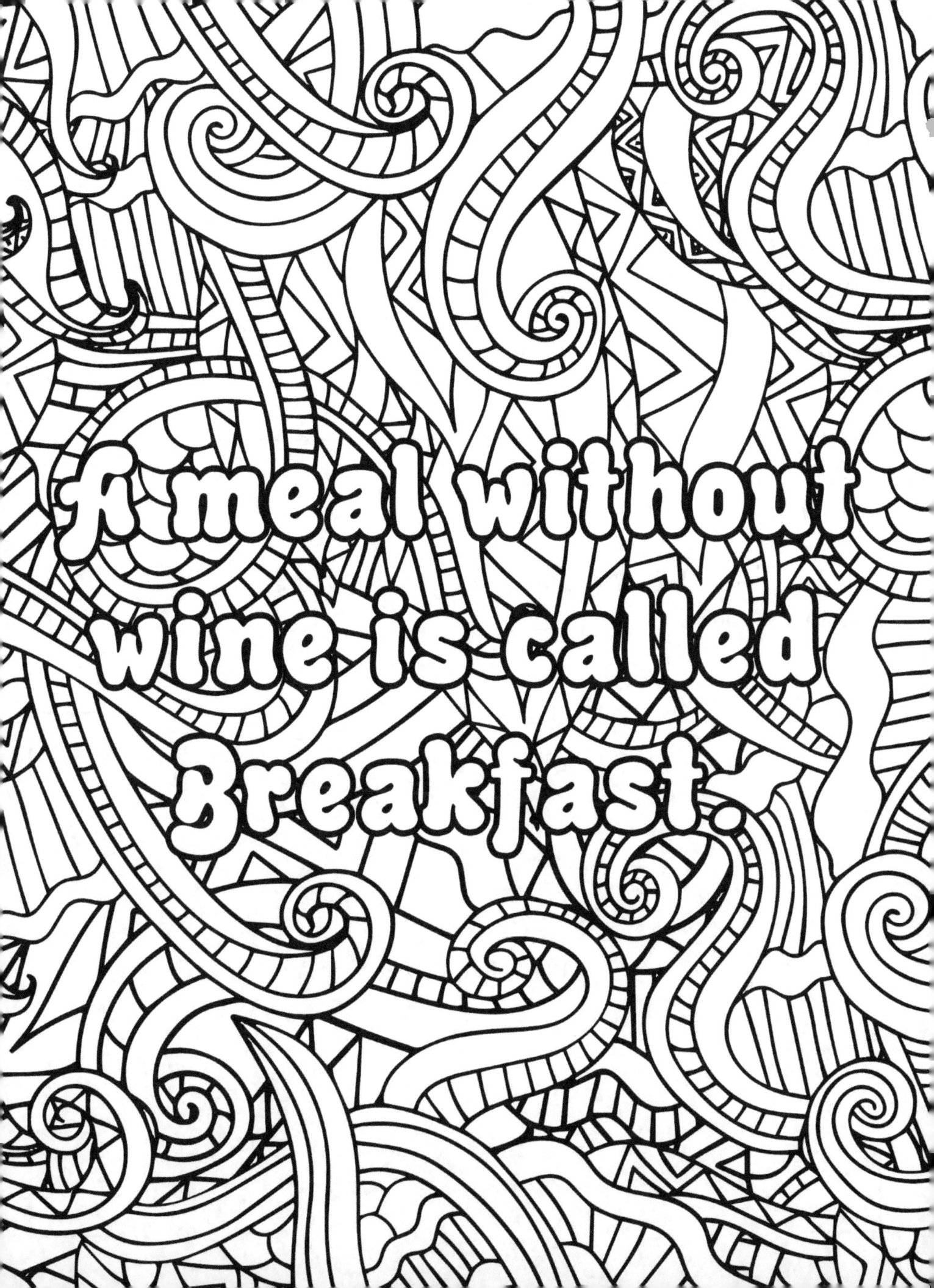

Name of Wine: _____

Region: _____

Type: _____ Vintage: _____

Vineyard: _____

Price: _____ Date: _____

Purchased/Received From: _____

Music Listened to: _____

Appearance: _____

Bouquet: _____

Taste: _____

Body:
|_____|_____|
Light   Medium   Full

Overall Rating:

☆ ☆ ☆ ☆ ☆

Additional Comments: _____
_____

Attach Wine Label Here

Name of Wine: _____

Region: _____

Type: _____ Vintage: _____

Vineyard: _____

Price: _____ Date: _____

Purchased/Received From: _____

Music Listened to: _____

Appearance: _____

Bouquet: _____

Taste: _____

Body: |——————————————————————|——————————————————————|

    Light   Medium   Full

Overall Rating:

☆ ☆ ☆ ☆ ☆

Additional Comments: _____

_____

Attach Wine Label Here

Learn Wine First Aid! Open the bottle to allow it to breathe. If it doesn't look like it's breathing, give it mouth-to-mouth.

Name of Wine: _____

Region: _____

Type: _____ Vintage: _____

Vineyard: _____

Price: _____ Date: _____

Purchased/Received From: _____

Music Listened to: _____

Appearance: _____

Bouquet: _____

Taste: _____

Body: |_____|_____|

Light   Medium   Full

Overall Rating:

☆ ☆ ☆ ☆ ☆

Additional Comments: _____
_____

Attach Wine Label Here

Name of Wine: _____

Region: _____

Type: _____ Vintage: _____

Vineyard: _____

Price: _____ Date: _____

Purchased/Received From: _____

Music Listened to: _____

Appearance: _____

Bouquet: _____

Taste: _____

Body: |——————————————————|——————————————————|

   Light   Medium   Full

Overall Rating:

☆ ☆ ☆ ☆ ☆

Additional Comments: _____

_____

Attach Wine Label Here

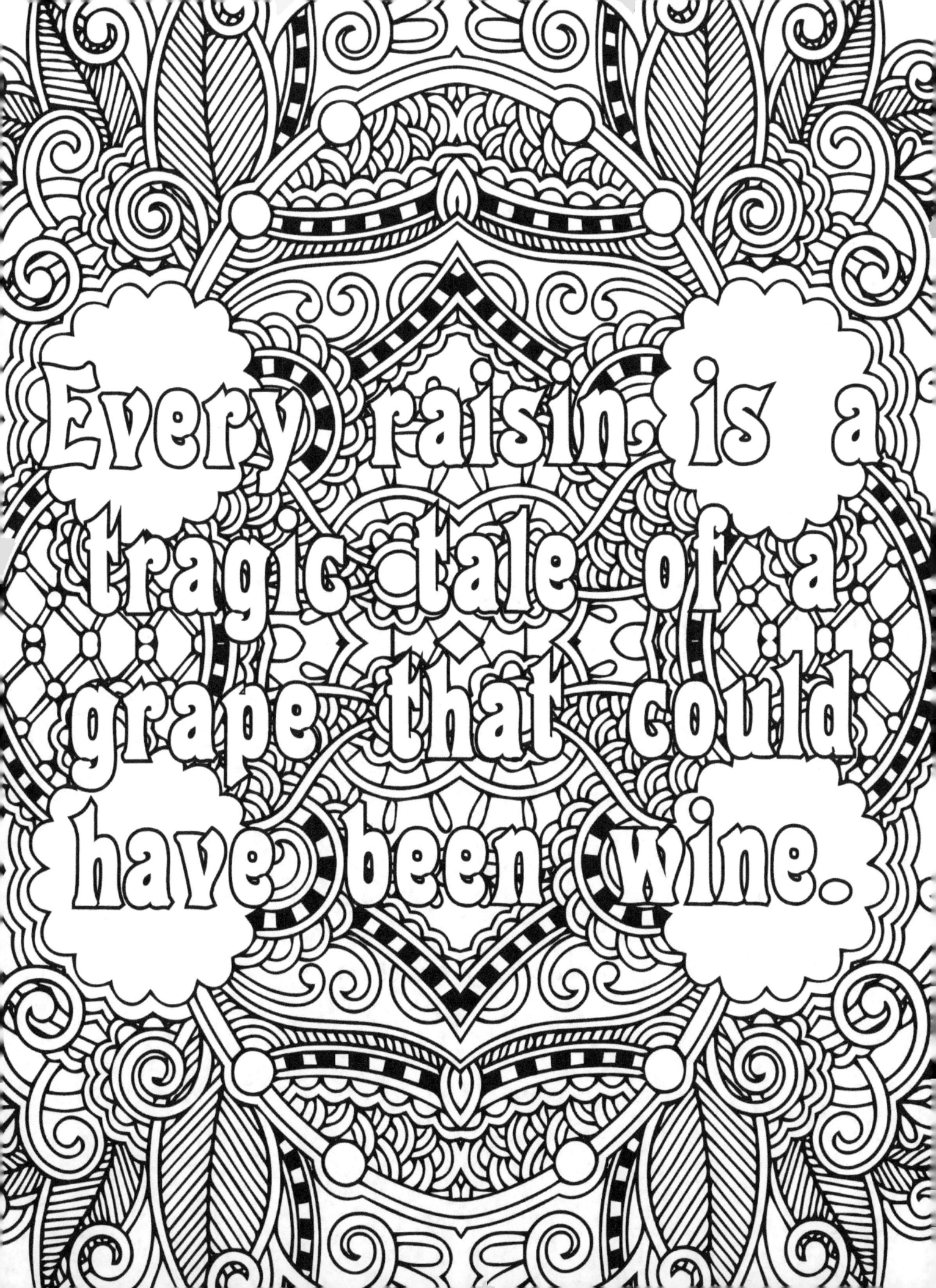

Every raisin is a tragic tale of a grape that could have been wine.

Name of Wine: _____

Region: _____

Type: _____ Vintage: _____

Vineyard: _____

Price: _____ Date: _____

Purchased/Received From: _____

Music Listened to: _____

Appearance: _____

Bouquet: _____

Taste: _____

Body: |——————————————|——————————————|

     Light   Medium   Full

Overall Rating:

☆ ☆ ☆ ☆ ☆

Additional Comments: _____
_____

Attach Wine Label Here

Name of Wine: _____

Region: _____

Type: _____ Vintage: _____

Vineyard: _____

Price: _____ Date: _____

Purchased/Received From: _____

Music Listened to: _____

Appearance: _____

Bouquet: _____

Taste: _____

Body: |—————————————|—————————————|

Light   Medium   Full

Overall Rating:

☆ ☆ ☆ ☆ ☆

Additional Comments: _____
_____

Attach Wine Label Here

Name of Wine: _____

Region: _____

Type: _____ Vintage: _____

Vineyard: _____

Price: _____ Date: _____

Purchased/Received From: _____

Music Listened to: _____

Appearance: _____

Bouquet: _____

Taste: _____

Body: |———————————————|———————————————|

Light   Medium   Full

Overall Rating:

☆ ☆ ☆ ☆ ☆

Additional Comments: _____

_____

Attach Wine Label Here

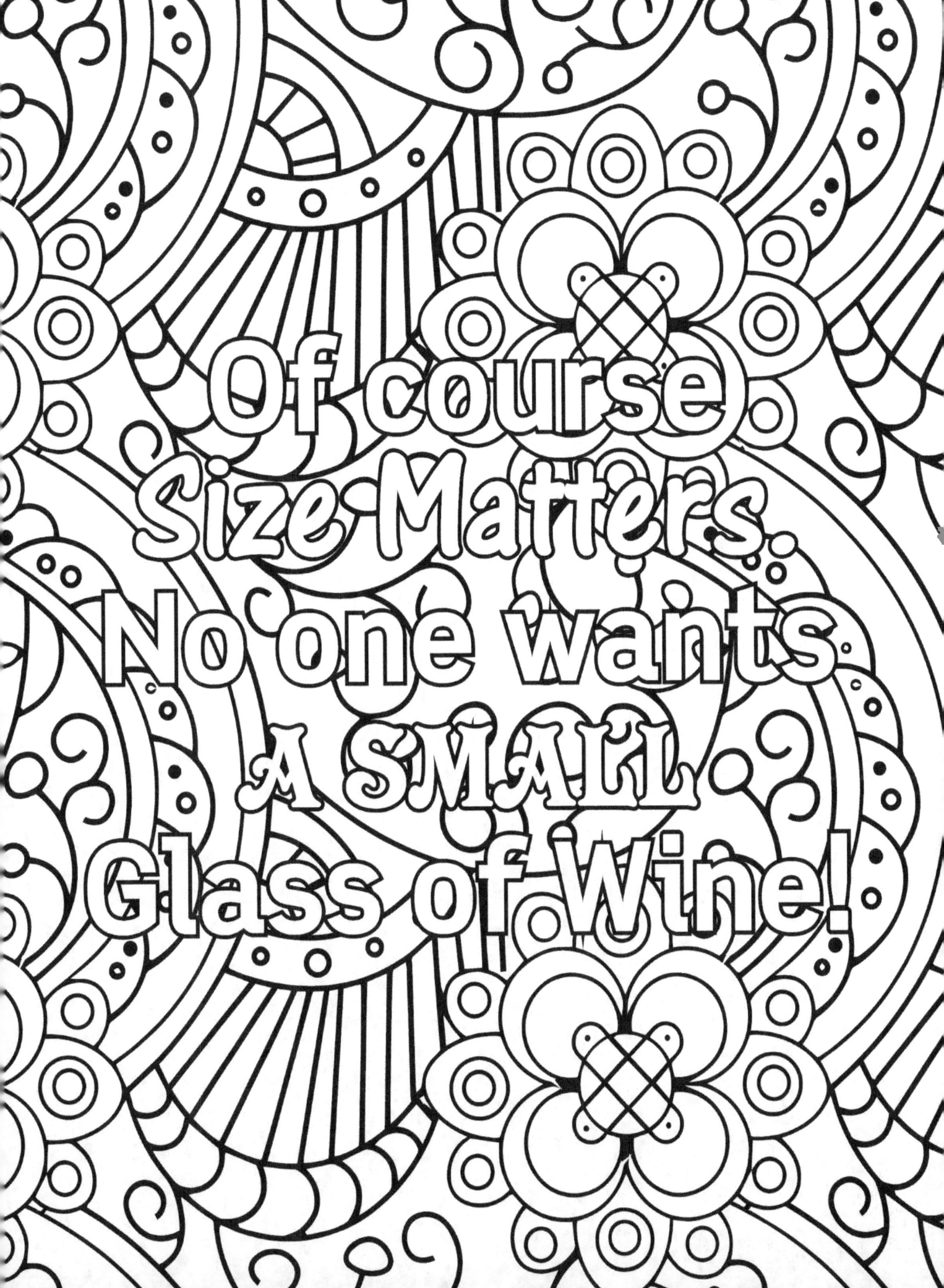

Of course Size Matters... No one wants A SMALL Glass of Wine!